THIS BOOK BELONGS TO

_____

I celebrated World Book Day® 2025
with this gift from my local bookseller and
Orion Children's Books.

THE
WOLF
TRIALS

Also by
KIRAN MILLWOOD HARGRAVE

KIRAN MILLWOOD HARGRAVE

THE
WOLF
TRIALS

A GEOMANCER BOOK

Orion

ORION CHILDREN'S BOOKS
First published in Great Britain in 2025 by Hodder & Stoughton

1 3 5 7 9 10 8 6 4 2

World Book Day® and the associated logo are the registered
trademarks of World Book Day® Limited.
Registered charity number 1079257 (England and Wales). Registered
company number 03783095 (UK).
Text copyright © Kiran Millwood Hargrave, 2025
Illustration copyright © Manuel Šumberac, 2025

ISBN 978 1 510 11342 8

Typeset in Duper OT by Jouve (UK), Milton Keynes
Printed and bound in Great Britain by Clays Ltd, Elcograf S.p.A.
The paper and board used in this book
are made from wood from responsible sources.

Orion Children's Books
An imprint of
Hachette Children's Group
Part of Hodder & Stoughton Limited
Carmelite House
50 Victoria Embankment
London EC4Y 0DZ

The authorised representative in the EEA is Hachette Ireland,
8 Castlecourt Centre, Dublin 15, D15 XTP3, Ireland (email: info@hbgi.ie)

An Hachette UK Company
www.hachette.co.uk
www.hachettechildrens.co.uk

CHAPTER ONE

It was a fearsome sight. Sand flew beneath mighty paws, cheers and howls filling the air, as Queen Seren rode out from her castle of broken boats on her wolf Tej. In her red sari, gold thread and jewellery glinting like armour from her black hair and brown wrists and bare ankles, with her spear slung across her back, she looked like a goddess or a demon.

Following her were the red-cloaked Ryders, her best warriors, also on wolfback: the wolf queen and her army. The entire castle came out to watch as they thundered into the distance, across the Lakes to greet her fleet before crossing the sea to defeat the uprising in the Marbled Hills. As soon as the sand settled and the racket faded, the crowd seemed to breathe out in relief. But no one was more relieved than Eira, the wolf queen's daughter, concealed among the skeletons of the ships' hulls that formed her mother's castle.

'Don't hurry back,' she whispered after the vanished

wolves, then turned and slid down the upturned hull, her clothes snagging on barnacles. She shouldn't have been watching the army leave. She shouldn't have been there at all.

Since birth, Eira had been kept a secret. Her mother claimed it was to protect her, but Eira thought Seren preferred being a queen to being a mother. Eira had been raised in caves beneath the castle, only a select and trusted few knowing of her existence. Most of whom had just ridden off.

Her mother visited every week when she wasn't away, teaching her of the nine realms: the languages, customs and histories. Eira recited her mother's different names, as she hit the sand and ran back to the sandstone cave.

'The Isles: Seren. The Marbled Hills: Thalassa. The Thawless Circle: Seqineq. Ural Mountains: Tsaritsa. Thousand Islands: Reyna. Hispania: Regina.' She ducked into the cave, forced to crawl by the low ceiling, her nostrils full of the sea that roared on the beach behind her. It was just as well she knew it so well: it was pitch black, and she didn't have a spare hand for a candle.

'Gesira Malai: Malika. Ægypt: Pharoah.' Eira reached the grate, a grid of metal that let air flow through and kept her in. She pushed it aside then pulled it back into place behind her, covering her tracks with a handful of sand.

In the dark of her room, she yanked off her jacket,

and threw herself into her unmade bed. 'The Mother Realm: Raani.'

She listened to her thumping heart, trying to slow her breathing, wiping sweat and sand from her hair and face with the blankets. Light leaked from beneath the closed door that led to the official corridors of her residence, soon blocked by a shadow. Someone knocked.

'Rajkumari? Princess?'

Eira smiled to herself. Amma. The nurse was softest on her, much kinder than the general or her other guardians, and easiest to fool since her sight had begun to fade. The room filled with light as she opened the door.

'Eira? Time to wake up.'

Trying to be convincing, Eira yawned and blinked up at the old woman, who was holding her usual cup of milk sweetened with honey. Eira took the cup while Amma fussed around the room.

The room was luxurious, as befitted the wolf queen's daughter. The cave was painted sky blue, with thick tapestries hung to keep the chill out, and an ornately carved desk and chair along one wall. An engraved mango-wood cupboard held her clothes, and the walls were lined with shelves full of scrolls of their realms' stories.

Any child would be glad to have such a splendid room, but it bored Eira. Other rooms were far more interesting: the armoury, where the general schooled her in combat; the map room, where her mother taught her history and languages; even the bathroom, where her bath was more like a lake, which she had filled with seawater so she could practise cold-water swimming. But this room was where she spent the most time: sleeping, eating, reading. At least, until she'd discovered the loose grate last year.

Amma was staring into her face with hazy eyes. 'You look pale. I'll add some turmeric paste to your porridge.' Turmeric paste was Amma's treatment for everything, from headaches and sore throats to nightmares and grumpiness. 'Your mother went this morning.'

'I know,' said Eira. 'I mean, she came to say goodbye last night.'

Amma patted her wrist. She seemed to think Eira cared when her mother left, which she didn't. 'The general has gone too. You'll be stuck with me for the next few weeks.'

Amma bustled out to prepare Eira's breakfast, and Eira flopped back on her pillows. She would have to get even better at acting, because her mother and the general's absence gave her an opportunity. Tomorrow the Wolf Trials would begin. And Eira was going to take part. And win.

CHAPTER TWO

It was Samhain in two weeks, when the spirit world and the mortal world rubbed closely, their boundaries frayed. It was also the night new Ryder apprentices were selected, at the end of the fortnight-long Wolf Trials. They took place every seven years, so this was Eira's only chance.

The Ryders were the key to her mother's success, trained from childhood to ride wolves and follow orders, to fight to the death if necessary. It all sounded terrible to Eira, except the first part. But if she competed as a Wolfling, and completed the trials, she would prove to her mother that she could look after herself. She would gain her freedom.

Feigning tiredness, she'd ordered Amma to let her sleep longer and crept through the grate as soon as Amma left. This time she took a different path, a tunnel that would take her to the closest person she had to a friend. The Forgiver was her proper title, but she never called Eira Princess and so Eira only ever called her Kore.

Kore was only a couple of years older than Eira. In Lakes parlance she was gifted, a famous oracle. Seren had captured her in the Marbled Hills and brought her back to not only see for her but also to forgive. Ruling a kingdom was a bloody business, full of sins, and it was Kore's role to forgive these sins before they were even committed.

Eira wriggled through the narrow gap that led into Kore's cave. She chose to live here instead of in the castle, preferring solitude.

Eira splashed through the rock pools that dotted the cave. She could smell incense and cooking. She found Kore still in her ceremonial robes, her antler headdress discarded, holding a skewer of meat over the dying flames.

'*Gods!*' said Kore in Hellenic. 'Don't you ever knock?'

'You don't have a door,' said Eira, sitting down. 'And for a seer you never seem to expect me.'

'Your mother had me up at the crack of dawn.' Kore pushed back her hair, leaving a streak of soot in the white. 'She wanted the full ceremony. Headdress, chanting, bloodletting, the lot.'

'Loves a show, does Seren.'

'Speaking of which,' said Kore, 'did I spot someone watching the leaving from the highest hull?'

Eira slid a piece of meat off Kore's skewer.

'Hey!'

'Need my strength,' said Eira, her mouth full. 'For tomorrow.'

Both of them fell silent. Eira thought of the cubs in the Lakes a few miles away. That was where the first trial took place. The task? To track a wolf.

As though she'd read her mind, Kore said, 'Let's say you compete. You've a good chance of completing the first trial; they just leave you to it, don't they? And the second, no spectators for that either. But what about the final trial? It's out there –' she gestured at the beach – 'for everyone to see. And what about Amma?'

'She's half blind.'

'I mean, while you're away. She'll notice her only charge isn't where she should be.'

Eira grinned. 'That's where you come in.'

Kore narrowed her pale eyes. 'I can't stand in for you.'

Eira looked between them, at Kore's white, almost see-through skin and her own, which was rich brown. She laughed. 'Obviously. But Amma's superstitious. She believes in you and she trusts you. Tell her you need me here while Seren's away. Tell her you need me to stay connected to her – that's a thing, isn't it?'

'Blood bond isn't like sending a letter,' said Kore sternly. 'It's a solemn art. The blood allows me to—'

'I don't know how it works, and neither does Amma. Please, Kore. I need this.'

'But what about when your mother's back? What if she punishes me?'

'I'll say it was all my idea.'

'It *is* all your idea.'

'And anyway, she won't punish you. You're her favourite.'

Kore looked at her, almost pityingly. 'I guess that's true.'

'So you'll do it?' Eira was buzzing with excitement. 'You'll cover for me?'

Kore took some ash from the fire and rubbed it between her fingers. She drew a smudgy circle on her wrist and Eira's, and pressed the circles together. 'With fire as my bond.' She caught hold of Eira's arm and pulled her in close. 'But if you die, I'll kill you.'

CHAPTER THREE

Death was a distinct possibility. In the twenty-one years since Seren had settled here and started the Wolf Trials, four souls had lost their lives. Many more were maimed or injured, but that was half the point. Only the strongest could become Ryders – and Seren wanted people she could mould, who would follow her anywhere. Eira disdained the Ryders for this blind faith.

She was back in her room, reading a scroll hidden beneath a wax tablet covered in Hellenic script. Amma was meant to be supervising, but she'd been called away to speak with Kore – the plan was underway.

When Amma returned, her brow furrowed, Eira knew Kore had been successful.

'I have news,' said Amma. 'I'm not sure what to feel about it.'

'What is it, Amma?' asked Eira, all innocence.

Amma sat down heavily on the chair next to her

and Eira listened as she explained, careful to keep her face under control. Kore had stuck to her word.

Amma rubbed her face tiredly. 'I'll visit, of course, but the Forgiver said it's best not to every day, to keep the blood bond strong. I wish I could ask your mother, or the general.'

'But surely my mother will have left the Forgiver instructions. We have to trust her.'

'Are you sure, *meri jaan*? You don't have to do anything you're uncomfortable with.'

Eira felt guilty, and ducked her head. 'I'm sure, Amma.'

Eira returned to Kore's cave, this time swathed in a headscarf to hide her appearance, accompanied by Amma and Dev, the most senior Ryder left behind. He had never seen Eira's face.

They walked through the upturned hulls of the castle, taking corridors that were forbidden to others. This was a place of halves. There were public markets, open classes where children and adults could learn the languages of the nine realms, dwellings where families lived in groups. Then there were private places reserved for Seren and her Ryders: the Hull Hall that served as Seren's throne room, with its map of the realms and crystal-inlaid throne, the wolf pens, and a network of tunnels that avoided prying eyes. *And then*, Eira thought, as they hurried through one such tunnel, *there is another world within this world*.

My world, where I am trapped.

They emerged on the beach, and walked in wild wind to the cave. Kore was waiting for them, her antler headdress in place, so she seemed half girl, half deer. Amma touched her feet in respect, and Dev followed suit.

Eira examined Kore through her veil. She played the part beautifully, looking otherworldly with her pale skin and white hair. Terrifying, even.

'Come, Rajkumari.' Kore held out her hand, and Eira stepped forward, trying not to laugh at Kore's deep tone. 'Do not fear. I will take care of you.'

'I will take the first watch,' said Dev, 'in case we were followed. But here is a dagger for protection. Keep it with you at all times, Princess.'

Eira nodded, sliding the dagger and its sheath into her belt.

Amma embraced her, looking nervous. 'When can I see you?'

Eira looked at Kore, deferentially.

Kore replied, 'I will send word.'

When Amma left, Dev took up his position outside the cave and Eira and Kore retreated to the shadows. Kore took off her headdress while Eira whooped quietly. 'Perfect performance!'

Kore was even paler than normal. 'Gods, I felt bad lying to Amma. I'd better be able to return you unscathed.'

Eira withdrew the dagger from its sheath. 'Well, almost.'

'What are you planning now?' asked Kore, eyeing it nervously. Eira smiled wickedly, and took her plait in hand. Kore gasped. 'You can't!'

Long hair was a big deal for the wolf queen, a sign of status. Seren usually wore hers loose, and it fell to her feet. Eira had never been allowed to cut her hair, but she wanted to be free of it for the Wolf Trials, and if it changed her appearance so much the better. She wrapped the plait around her wrist, pulled it taut, and sawed. The dagger slid through easily, as sharp as a wolf's fang, and Eira felt her hair brush her ears, the plait heavy in her hand.

Kore stared at her, aghast.

'Don't just stand there.' Eira grinned. 'Tidy up the back, will you?'

CHAPTER FOUR

The path to the Lakes stretched out before them. Somewhere in that wilderness was a huge enclosure where the wolf cubs roamed. 'Cubs' was a misleading word: they were a year old, fierce and untamed. But the task was to find and mark one.

Eira lined up outside the main gate to the castle with twenty-eight other competitors; she was among the youngest, and the oldest looked about fifteen. He would be old enough to remember the last Wolf Trials seven years ago, when two children had died in a riptide. But he looked determined, his eyes fixed on the horizon.

The girl and boy either side of Eira looked less sure. The boy was trembling, and the girl anxiously scanned the crowd gathered to see the Wolflings off. Eira wondered which of the grown-ups were her parents, and whether they had forced her to enter.

Amma was not there. 'Children should be protected, not trained to kill,' she said. It was the only thing she disagreed with Eira's mother about.

Eira tugged on the neck of her tunic. They were all dressed in the Wolflings uniform: black tunic and leggings, shoes tied up their legs with silver cord. Each of them had been supplied with a length of rope, a knife, a flint for starting fires, and a pouch of red dye. They had to get close enough to mark a wolf with the dye, using their symbol. Eira had chosen a bat because she had been forced to live in the dark for so long; she had practised it in the sand of Kore's cave.

'Maybe you should do an earthworm instead,' said Kore, squinting at it, but Eira had simplified the design until she could draw it in two seconds.

No one seemed to know who she was, but now was the moment of truth. A murmur came from the crowd gathered around them, which parted to reveal five Ryders on wolfback.

Eira had seen sea wolves before, but it was different seeing them like this, in their battle regalia. They seemed much bigger and much, much scarier. They stood nearly as tall and broad as horses, covered in thick fur, the white tips of their fangs visible.

Dev was at the head of the pack on his wolf, his red cloak draped around his shoulders, his spear slung across his back. He was followed by two other Ryders Eira had never seen, but the fourth was Ani. *Gods*. Eira ducked her head. Ani had worked as one of her mother's serving girls when she was young, but

Ani wouldn't have seen her since . . . Eira counted. Ani would have stopped working as a maid when Eira was four. Eira only remembered her because of her striking green eyes.

She looked up in time to see those green eyes pass over her without a flicker of recognition. Eira rubbed her cropped head gratefully. Eira had kept a few strands at the front long, attaching a bead to the end. It was like a tether, a connection to her past.

'Wolflings!' Dev boomed. 'You are about to undertake a dangerous and hallowed mission. All of us who ride before you have done what you must do in order to win the honour of the red cloak.' The Ryders let out a short *ahru* of respect. 'It will not be easy, but nothing worth having is simple. You will risk your lives, but the prize is immeasurable. To serve Seren is a privilege beyond measure, and to bond with a wolf something few experience.'

It was easy to tell who was here because they wanted to be. The boy next to Eira trembled worse than ever.

'You don't have to go, you know,' murmured Eira.

He jumped and looked at her, sweaty-faced. 'My mother was a Ryder.'

'We don't have to do what our mothers say.'

He frowned. 'Yes we do.'

Dev spoke again. 'You have all you require. You have until sunset on the second day to mark your wolf. Anyone who has not marked a wolf by then shall fail the trial. Understood?'

'Yes!' shouted the oldest boy, the others following suit less enthusiastically.

'Ani will come and collect your marks.'

Eira ground her teeth. Of course it would be Ani.

Ani moved along the line with a long scroll. Each child made their handprint on the parchment, and next to it drew their symbol. If they were successful, they would receive a brooch with this symbol on it. Eira watched: a sun, a moon, stars – these were common but so long as no one in the same group chose them, allowed. The oldest boy drew a snake, and Eira smiled to herself, remembering Kore's comment about the worm. The girl next to her drew an oak leaf with a shaking finger. And then Ani stood before her.

Keeping her head lowered, Eira pressed her hand into the dye, and then on to the parchment, leaving a palm print. Then she drew her bat beside it. It didn't turn out bad.

'Interesting.' Ani's green eyes squinted, and then widened. 'You remind me of someone.'

'Ani?' Dev was behind her, still on wolfback. Ani carried on along the line. The boy next to Eira drew a wave, with a lot of extra wobbles. As Ani moved out of earshot Eira leaned over and said, 'You could say you don't want to do it. It should be of your own free will.'

The boy shook his head jerkily. 'I have to. Mother

said I have to try, or else I'll bring shame on the family. She completed the Wolf Trials in the Mother Realm. An original Ryder, like Hajay's mother.' The boy pointed at the oldest boy.

Eira shrugged. This didn't impress her. 'And you are?'

'Ish. Ishan.'

She tightened the laces around her calves. Ani had finished collecting their marks and rolled the scroll tightly, handing it to Dev before swinging herself back up on to her own wolf. Eira thought she felt her eyes lingering on her, but she focused on the horizon.

'At my signal the Wolf Trials shall begin!' called Dev. He raised his arm. The sky was ablaze with the sunrise behind him.

Eira's heart beat hard as she readied herself, her eyes fixed on his arm. The crowd, the wolves, even the sea seemed to hold its breath. And then Dev's arm sliced down, and the Wolflings began to run.

CHAPTER FIVE

The oldest boy, Hajay, took the lead. Eira stayed near the back with Ish and a couple of others. They could stay together for now: it was a few miles to the enclosure, where they would have to split up to track the wolves.

With every stride, Eira felt her body relax. She was out; she was free. She could break away and keep running, never come back. But she'd thought this before, even tried to run away a couple of years ago. The wolves had caught up with her, brought her back. The only way to outpace a wolf was on a wolf.

After the first hard ascent, the view opened up below them. Eira stopped, Ish bumping into her back. But Eira was transfixed by the view. Their hill stood taller than those nearby, and lakes shone in little pools of silver like dropped coins at the foot of the rolling hills. Further away were the sharper teeth of low mountains. And there – Eira squinted. Was that . . . ?

'The wall!' shouted Ish, pointing. Over the next hill was a thick black blockade made of wooden stakes set close together so the cubs could not escape. Larger children like Hajay would have to climb over, but she was hoping to be able to save her energy, and slip through.

The small group plunged down the hillside. They made it to the base without injury, and refilled their flasks from the lake. Eira stoppered her flask with charcoal from Kore's fire, which would help purify the water.

'Clever,' said a voice, and Eira looked up to see the girl who'd been beside her on the starting line. She was flushed from running. 'I'm Meri.'

'Ei— Esta. And this is Ish.'

'I know Ish,' said Meri. She seemed less nervous now she was away from the castle. 'But I've never seen you around.'

Eira shrugged. 'Big place.' Before Meri could comment further Eira shoved her flask back into her belt, and said to Ish, 'Come on.'

Reluctantly, he broke into a jog, and followed her up the next hill, to the wall. Eira let him fall behind, pushing herself so she reached it first. It felt threatening up close, stretching high above her head. The stakes were cut from the tallest trees, the gaps between them barely a handspan. Eira measured herself against the gap. She would just fit.

Ish and Meri caught up, panting, but Eira was

ready to leave them both behind. 'Well, good luck! See you at the second trial.'

Without a backward glance, she forced herself inside the enclosure. The landscape inside was the same, but the wall both blocked and trapped the wind, snatching at Eira's single braid and then dropping instantly. The heather shivered and stilled eerily. There were no wolves in sight.

She got her bearings – the sea was to the west, hills to the east, and ahead the grey teeth of mountains, their lower reaches fringed with trees. She thought she saw movement in the shadows cast by the trees. A Wolfling, or a wolf cub? Either way, that was where she needed to go. The wolves, cut off from the sea that was their natural habitat, would head for forests, for caves.

Eira ran along the ridge, making for the forested foothills. She passed a tangle of brambles, paused to pick the last bitter fruits and swallowed some down, grimacing, storing the rest. She checked behind her. She thought she could make out Ish and Meri walking together. She hoped they wouldn't get hurt, or worse.

Not your problem, Eira, she told herself.

She turned and continued at pace. The sun was at the highest point of the sky, but it would begin to get dark in a few hours, maybe five at most. Eira needed to get to the trees, start a fire, fashion a torch so she could continue the hunt at night, and not become hunted herself.

CHAPTER SIX

Eira just beat the sunset. She reached the trees as the sky turned pink. At least it hadn't rained, and the sky was still clear. That meant a cold night, but she wouldn't have to contend with wet clothes. She walked deeper into the forest until she found a natural clearing, free of pawprints. She collected branches and dry leaves from the ground, marked off a firepit with stones and lit the wood with her flint. The wolf cubs would stay clear of the smoke and light.

When this was done, she once again broke the treeline to fish in the lake. She waded into the freezing water, mastering her tremble by breathing deeply. She stood as still as a stork in the shallows, her hand trailing in the water. As her back began to ache, a couple of fish began to flick around her fingertips, drawn by the ripples.

Eira was patient, waiting until a larger one came to investigate. When she felt it nibble her index finger, she batted it into the air. It flapped on the mossy bank and she withdrew the dagger Dev had given her, and killed it.

She dressed, shivering, and cooked it over the now-crackling fire, eating quickly, not wanting the smell to draw any wolves. She kept the skeleton and innards and buried them for bait tomorrow. Then she washed her hands in the lake. The stars were out now, the dark around her unbroken but for her fire and another speck of light in the distance. She hoped Ish and the others were safe.

Eira climbed a nearby tree, a forked ash, and settled into the V of its boughs. She tied the rope around her waist and the thick branch beneath her, so it would hold her if she fell. Her mother's lessons had prepared her well. She thought of all the nights she had spent underground in stale air, in her gilded cage. Her last waking thought was this: *I'm here. I'm out. I'm free.*

Eira's first waking thought was: *wolf.* Her eyes snapped open but darkness was pressing in – it was the dead of night, and in the thick of the tree not even the stars shone on her. Then she heard it again: the rustle of leaves, the breaking of twigs. A big wolf cub, by the sounds – brave too, to approach a burning fire, for hers was still throwing flames high into the air. When it was below her, she untied herself and jumped, ready to defend herself—

'Argh!'

'Gods!' she shouted. 'What are you *doing* sneaking around?'

Ish was sprawled in the firelight, wincing in pain as he sat up.

'I was hungry,' he said. 'I saw the fire and thought someone might be here.'

Resisting the urge to roll her eyes, Eira helped him to his feet. 'You know we're meant to work alone, right? We can't share a wolf.'

'I know,' said Ish, rubbing his shoulder.

'Stay here,' she sighed. 'Stick close to the fire, all right?'

He nodded, his belly rumbling audibly.

Eira returned to the lake, muttering to herself about bad mothers and useless boys and lost sleep. She returned with another two fishes, gutted and cleaned, and Ish watched in awe as she cooked them over the fire. He ate his and half hers in a few bites.

He yawned widely, lying back on the ground. 'Thank you.'

'You can't sleep here,' said Eira.

'Why not?'

'For one, you need to wash your hands, or the wolves will smell the food and come. For two, this is my camp.'

'Could I stay tonight? I'll go as soon as it gets light, I promise.'

Eira ground her teeth. 'Fine. But we have to sleep in the trees. You stoke the fire.'

Ish beamed as he added logs to keep it burning through what remained of the night. Eira climbed back to her spot in the ash tree and watched him. He looked around for her when he was done, and started to climb up to her.

'Find your own tree at least!' she snapped.

Ish ignored her, climbing up to the bough across from her and tying his own rope as she had.

'You really shouldn't be here, you know.'

'I know,' he said.

'Why did you agree to do this?'

'I want my mother to be proud of me.'

Eira wondered what that would feel like. Ish was soon snoring softly. Eira closed her eyes, and drifted once more into dreams.

CHAPTER SEVEN

It was dark when Eira woke, but she could just see the lake through the trees, its surface starting to pinken. Ish was still asleep.

Eira untied herself and leaped lightly down from her perch. The fire was smouldering, and she coaxed it into full flame again before walking deeper into the forest. As she'd expected, the sweet chestnut trees were full of fruit. She filled her pockets, then returned to camp and placed them in the fire to roast.

Ish slept through the smell of them cooking, but despite her better judgement Eira saved him a handful wrapped in leaves. She dug up the bones, and wrapped them in leaves, too. Then, determined not to feel bad for leaving him, she struck out for the mountain.

She reached the foot within hours. The trees had thinned and thick clouds threatened rain. Ahead stretched the mountain, trees giving way to valerian and gorse, and caves. Eira's belly flipped. She was not so foolhardy as to corner a wolf in its cave. Sticking to the treeline, she withdrew the fishbones from her belt and unwrapped them.

The smell was strong and sweet, the innards glossy. Eira placed them on the ground, and then tied her rope in a loose noose, encircling the bait. She ran the rest of the rope over a nearby bough, and clambered up beside it. The tree was a pine, and she was well concealed. Eira withdrew the pouch of dye, and waited.

It did not take long for movement to draw her eye. From an upper cave, a large, pale shape emerged, glowing in the grey light. Her first sighting of a wild wolf.

Though technically still cubs, the wolves were nearly full grown. Eira thought this one would stand higher than her head. It moved closer, zigzagging towards the smell, and then Eira spotted something on its side. Blood? Was it hurt?

But as it came closer, she realised it was marked. She swore and squinted. A snake. Hajay had selected this wolf cub.

The wolf was still slinking closer, picking its way across the boulders. She had time to save her bait. She jumped down and gathered the bones and guts back into a tangle of leaves.

A snarl made her look up.

The wolf was suddenly there, impossibly close. In two bounds, it would be upon her. Eira stood carefully, dropping the bones. She began to back away, but the smell was all over her, and she knew she was a more appealing prospect than some leftovers. Fear filled her. The wolf's eyes were amber, its fur sandy white. She could tell it was male. It was holding its left front paw oddly, and Eira realised it was injured. Its lips peeled back, showing white fangs long as Eira's fingers.

Though her entire body wanted to run, she knew that was not how to escape a wolf. If she acted like prey, the wolf would attack. Clasping her dagger, she spread her arms, and bared her own teeth in a growl. She began to back away.

The cub limped closer. It was afraid, in pain. A dangerous combination.

It reached the remains of the fish. Eira could almost sense it making a decision – an easy, smaller meal, or a larger kill with the risk of being hurt. Her breath was coming hard; she couldn't control it. The wolf looked right into her eyes once more – then lowered its head to eat.

Eira ran for her life. She ran blindly, stumbling into the thicker forest, checking back over her shoulder to see if the wolf was following. Brambles tore at her clothes, and she was going so fast that when something came hurtling through the trees towards her, there was no time to avoid it. Eira tumbled to the ground. But it wasn't a wolf.

'Oof! You idiot!' said a harsh voice. 'Watch where you're going!'

Winded, she peered up to see Hajay glaring down

at her. 'You . . . were . . . running . . . too . . .'

The boy preened. 'Just keeping warm.'

Eira struggled to sit up. 'Why . . . are . . . you . . . here?'

Hajay made no move to help her and tapped the side of his head. 'Er, it's called the Wolf Trials?'

Eira gulped in air, looking over her shoulder. 'I saw your mark . . . on a wolf back there.'

'That was my first attempt. It was damaged, so I'm going to get one fresh.'

Eira bristled. 'You're just going to leave it?'

Hajay scoffed. 'Gods, hardly Ryder material, are you?'

'Ryders are meant to care about their wolves,' said Eira hotly.

'They're meant to be their masters, not their friends.' Hajay narrowed his eyes. 'Who are you anyway?'

'Esta,' said Eira.

'Never heard of you. Maybe see you in the next trial.' He curled his lip. 'Though I doubt it.'

CHAPTER EIGHT

Eira took shelter in a clutch of pines as the rain sluiced down. She couldn't get the injured cub out of her head, its eyes full of pain and fear. The dye couldn't be washed away, but if there was a way to turn the mark into a bat, she would do it. As she watched the droplets striking the ground, Eira had an idea. A bat was a step too far . . . but a wave?

When the worst of the rain abated, Eira retraced her steps back to her camp, her mind whirring. She was unsurprised to find Ish still there, uselessly holding his arms over the fire to try to keep it from going out. Though she rolled her eyes, she was secretly thrilled. She needed Ish on board for her plan.

'Thanks for the chestnuts,' said Ish, his teeth chattering as he watched her gather birch twigs, which would still burn when wet, and add them to the fire.

She looked at him, considering, and he looked up at her dolefully. 'Are you sure you want to be here?

You could just leave, go back to the castle, say you couldn't do it.'

'I can't,' he said desperately. 'My mother will never forgive me if I embarrass her.'

Eira sighed. It was against her better judgement, but at least now she could help the hurt wolf. 'Listen, I have an idea.'

She explained about Hajay and the cub with the mark on its side. 'I think you could make it a wave. And then he would become your wolf.'

'But what about you?'

'I'll track another. I just need more fish.'

'Who are you?' he asked in admiration.

Eira tried not to preen – she didn't want to be like Hajay.

The journey back to where Eira had encountered the wolf was slower, both because of Ish and because the ground was becoming muddy. The day was starting to darken when they finally reached the treeline, the caves barely visible through the gloom.

'Do we light a fire?' asked Ish, his teeth chattering.

Eira shook her head. 'We want the wolves to come to us. Tonight is our last chance.'

He nodded solemnly. 'What do I do?'

Eira resisted the urge to say *Stay out of the way*. 'Fetch my rope. I don't want to hurt the wolf more.' She eyed the flowers she'd noticed before. 'We need another way to track him.'

By the time everything was ready, it was dark and Eira's hands were covered in fish scales. She and Ish were in the pine tree she'd climbed the night before, silent and alert.

They didn't have to wait long.

Two round lights, like small moons, appeared in a cave ahead of them. Eira's pulse quickened. It wasn't the same cave, and as the creature emerged into the rain, she saw immediately it was not the same wolf. It was brown and smaller than the injured one, thinner muzzled – a female. But this worked. Eira needed to mark her wolf, and even if this one ate all the fish, they had two more ready to go.

Ish shifted, his breath coming in pants, and Eira hushed him sharply. *Don't move*, she willed him.

Three skinned fish stuffed with roots waited beyond the treeline. The cub halted a little way off, scanning her surroundings, but she couldn't smell Eira and Ish because of the rain. Only the fish. She waited longer, and then, deciding it was safe, trotted to the fish. She sniffed them, and Eira held her breath. Would she smell the valerian? Did valerian even have a smell?

But the wolf ate a fish, sinking down on to her belly. As she chewed, Eira spotted another two eyes higher up the mountain. The same cave as yesterday. As the wolf stepped out, the scudding clouds parted, and a sliver of moonlight hit its pelt, making it glow. Eira's heart pounded. He looked majestic, but she could feel his pain from here, and winced as he made his limping way down the mountain.

The she-wolf smelled him. She'd finished two fish and whipped around, her lips peeled back, growling. The injured wolf cub hesitated. He was far larger than her, and unhurt there would be no match. But his paw was swollen, lifted even higher than the night before. He loped closer. She growled louder, arched over the remaining fish. The hurt wolf was panting, but his eyes were determined. He was hungry, unable to hunt. He readied himself to pounce—

The female wolf gave up. She turned and bounded into the forest, passing below Ish and Eira. Eira hoped the valerian wouldn't take long to act. She watched as the injured wolf sniffed the fish, and swallowed it in one bite. He searched the ground for more.

Eira threw her remaining fish towards the boulders. The wolf cub started, looking up and around, his fur on end. But he couldn't see them. He took the bait. He limped to the two fish and ate them too. Then, looking pitiful in the falling rain, he hobbled back to his cave.

'What now?' asked Ish triumphantly.

'Now we wait.'

CHAPTER NINE

Eira counted to a thousand in every language she knew. They were soaked through, and she had to unpeel her fingers from the branches one by one and blow on them to bring back any feeling.

'All right,' she said at last. 'We can go.'

'You're sure they're asleep?' asked Ish.

'Sleepy at least. And we need to be outside the wall at sunup. We can't waste any more time.' She climbed down to the sodden ground. Her boots filled with mud and she grimaced. Not long, and she would be back at the castle. She could get a warm bath, wash her hair . . .

'I'll see you outside the wall,' she said to Ish.

'Aren't you coming?'

'Gods!' snapped Eira. 'All you have to do is turn the snake into waves.'

Ish's face fell.

Eira gave a snort of impatience. 'Give me your dye. Just stay here. And don't get eaten by anything.'

She ran towards the hurt wolf's cave. The boulders were slick and she fell a couple of times, bruising her legs and jarring her shoulder. She stopped at the entrance, dagger in hand, and peered into the darkness.

At the back of the cave, curled up like a dog and glowing like a slice of moonbeam, was the cub. Eira kicked a couple of stones into the cave, the noise echoing. The wolf didn't move. Eira sighed in relief – the valerian had done its job. Her mother took it sometimes, to help her sleep, and wolf healers used it when setting bones.

Eira crept closer to the sleeping wolf. It was lying on its left side, its injured paw held at an odd angle in the air, the snake clear against its pale haunches. She sank to her knees beside it, feeling an odd sensation in her chest. Affection. She reached out and twined her fingers through its fur. It was coarse and damp from the rain, and so thick her entire hand disappeared into it. Then Eira withdrew her hand and covered her fingers in dye, working quickly.

She squinted. It wasn't perfect, but it would do.

'You'll get the help you need,' she murmured, resting her hand lightly on the wolf's muzzle. He whimpered in his sleep, as though he understood.

'It's done,' said Eira.

Ish had managed not to be eaten, and was waiting wide-eyed at the treeline. To her horror, his eyes filled with tears.

'Thank you,' he croaked, and threw himself forward, hugging her tightly.

Eira struggled free. She didn't, as a rule, hug.

'You can thank me by getting to the wall safely.'

'I know.' Ish beamed. 'Shall I come with you? Help with your wolf?'

'No,' said Eira quickly. 'I'll see you at the wall.'

She made sure he was really gone before following the path the female cub had taken. She found her slumped in the shadows of a thick clump of oak trees. At first when she saw the scarlet, Eira didn't understand. But . . . it was in the unmistakable shape of an oak leaf.

Eira swore. Meri had marked the wolf. Eira kicked a nearby tree and felt pain ricochet up her leg. She slumped down beside the wolf, cradling her head in her hands. The rain had finally stopped, and as the clouds moved Eira checked the position of the stars. She had maybe four hours before sunrise. Not enough time to mark a wolf and reach the wall.

If only she hadn't gone to the cave for Ish, she probably would have got here first. If she had focused on trapping a wolf instead of babysitting him, she definitely would have. Now she would return without a marked wolf, and her trial would be over.

It was a long and miserable walk back to the wall. She was in no rush – she'd failed after all – but she still reached the boundary just before the sun rose. She forced herself through the gap. There were about twenty children waiting on the other side. Eira could see Hajay and Ish, and Meri. She wasn't to know she'd stolen Eira's wolf, but she must know she'd taken advantage of someone else's plan.

'Easy,' Hajay was saying to no one in particular. 'I trapped the biggest one.'

Ish made his way to Eira. 'Are you all right? Did you find her?'

'Yes,' said Eira. She wanted to lash out at him, but didn't want to make a scene. 'Someone else had marked her.'

Ish gasped. 'No! Esta, I'm so sorr—'

'Just leave it will you?' she snapped. 'Stay away from me.'

Distraction came as the sun rose over the horizon: the five judges on wolfback, riding from the direction of the castle. Eira's heart gave a dull pang. Soon her failure would be public knowledge.

Hajay puffed out his chest. 'Here they come!'

But it was not him who walked out to meet them. It was Ish.

CHAPTER TEN

'What's that pip doing?' asked Hajay, watching Ish come to halt in front of Dev's enormous wolf. Ish's knees were visibly knocking, but he stood straight. They were out of earshot, but Hajay strode towards them, and Eira followed.

Dev was leaning down, frowning. As Hajay and Eira reached them, he looked up, and Ish pointed.

'Her. Esta. She marked my wolf for me.'

Dev dismounted. 'Is this true?'

Eira glanced at Ish.

'Tell him,' he said. 'You deserve to be in the second trial.'

'Yes,' she said. She felt Hajay's eyes on her.

Dev looked down at her sternly. 'This has never happened before. There are three days before the next trial. I shall send a messenger pigeon to General Shivani for guidance. Report to the armoury in two days' time for our verdict.'

Eira's heart stuttered at the mention of her

mother's second in command. She nodded. Ani's eyes were latched on to her. She wished she still had long hair, and could hide her face.

Eira went straight to Kore's cave, and found the Forgiver pacing around her lit fire.

'There you are! Dev's been here; he wanted to see you.'

Eira snatched up her headscarf and wound it around her, masking her mouth and nose. 'Why?'

'Some girl made a fuss at the first trial,' said Kore with narrowed eyes. 'Marked someone else's wolf for them and didn't manage to mark one for herself. He wanted to use your blood bond to find out where your mother was, so he could send a pigeon asking what to do. I said I thought it sounded like immediate disqualification—'

'You didn't!' Eira gasped.

'So it *was* you.' Kore glared even harder.

Eira grinned inside her headscarf. 'Is he coming back?'

Kore shook her head, and Eira removed the disguise. 'Don't look so pleased with yourself. I managed to convince him you were sleeping and couldn't be disturbed, but I don't think this is going to work, Eira. Too many things could go wrong.'

'We can't stop now,' said Eira. 'Let's make sure Amma sees me and Dev can visit, so everyone knows I'm where I'm meant to be.'

Kore threw up her hands, exasperated. 'Remind me why I'm helping you again?'

'Because you love me,' said Eira, punching her friend gently on the shoulder. 'And admit it, you love a good story.'

Rolling her eyes, Kore fetched her kettle and put it over the fire. 'Come on then, tell me.'

Two days later, as ordered, Eira went to the armoury. It was strange going there undisguised, taking the public route through the market, passing the guards at the door and giving her name as Esta. She found Dev already there, practising hand-to-hand combat with Ani. Eira paused on the threshold, watching them spin and kick, leap and punch. It was brutal, and graceful, and terrifying.

Dev spotted her, and raised his hand to stop the fight.

'We heard from General Shivani,' he said. 'This is unorthodox, and you understand that we do not condone your actions.'

Eira hung her head, feeling her heartbeat in her ears.

'But we agreed your actions demonstrated a willingness to put the interests of others above your own. We will allow you to proceed, but if there are any further breaches of protocol, you will be disqualified. Understood?'

Eira nodded.

'Very well. See you tomorrow for the second trial.'

'Wait,' said Eira, and Dev looked down at her, surprised. 'What will happen to Ish? The boy whose mark I used.'

Dev waved his hand as though swatting aside a fly. 'He returned to his family in disgrace.'

Eira swallowed. 'And the cub I marked? Is he healing well?'

'Wolfling,' said Dev hotly, 'your questions will be answered tomorrow. We have places to be.' He swept from the room without a backward glance, but Ani stayed.

After a long pause, she said, 'I'm sure I know you.'

Eira met her gaze. 'I'm sorry,' she said. 'I can't think how.'

'Ani!' Dev's voice barked from outside, and Ani went, frowning to herself.

CHAPTER ELEVEN

Eighteen Wolflings met at the sandstone steps. Before them was the largest entrance to the network of tunnels that underlay the entire coastline. In this vast maze, their wolves waited, so they could attempt the second trial. To tame a wolf.

'You have all you need,' said Dev, holding up each piece of equipment as he named it. 'Weapon. Rope. Flint. Torch. Meat. Bell. Whistle. This final item is crucial. If you blow the whistle three times, it is a forfeit. We will come and extract you, and you will not become a Ryder.

'You have one day. Twelve hours to gain the trust of the wolf. They must willingly follow you from the tunnels. There is no light, so time will be marked by a drum – one beat every hour. It is up to you to keep count.'

Eira had scanned the crowd, but there was no sign of Ish. She hoped his mother had not been too unkind about what happened. She was standing beside Meri again, who seemed less nervous, more determined.

'Ready?' she murmured to Eira, and Eira nodded. She was still annoyed about Meri marking her wolf, but it had worked out in the end. She was excited to see the pale wolf.

The five judges split up, and took groups of Wolflings to the tunnels five at a time. Eira was in the final group, with Meri and Hajay, being led by Ani. She loitered at the back as Ani took them down the steps. The day above was cool, and in the caves it was freezing, the air smelling of seawater. By the light of Ani's torch, they walked through the wide tunnel and turned off into a narrower one. Their shuffling footsteps echoed off the walls.

'Here,' said Ani, standing by a wooden door marked with a snake. Hajay squared his shoulders and pushed it open, disappearing inside.

The next door was marked with an oak leaf. Trembling but resolute, Meri nodded.

'Good luck,' she said to Eira, and vanished inside.

Ani and Eira walked on in silence, until they reached a third door marked with a bat. Eira's door. Eira made to push it open, but Ani barred her way.

'I think I know who you are.'

Eira froze, her hand against the wood.

'If I'm right, I should tell someone. It's a dereliction of my duty to do anything else.' Eira kept her face blank, but her pulse was racing. 'But here's the problem – I don't agree with a child being kept hidden, even if it is to protect them. And if I don't agree, I shouldn't help it happen.'

Eira listened, barely breathing.

'And if I'm the only one who knows, then maybe it's all right for me not to notice.' Ani grimaced. 'But if anything were to happen, to this person I think you are, then the consequences would be dire. Not only for you, but for those charged with your care. So I am asking . . . I am beseeching you . . . not to take any risks beyond the obvious. Do not endanger others' lives by endangering your own. If you must use your whistle, use it. Do you understand me?'

Eira chewed her tongue. She didn't know whether to trust Ani.

'Do you understand me, Rajkumari?'

Eira looked at her, into the searching green eyes. 'I understand.'

She pushed open the door.

It closed, hard, behind her. The darkness was immediate and absolute. Eira stretched her eyes wide, but there was no light for them to drink in. She felt for her flint and torch, struck the flint against the wall and nursed the spark in the brush of her torch, blowing on it and sheltering it from the sucking cold until it caught. It threw a meagre circle of flickering light around her. Somewhere nearby, the pale wolf waited.

Different routes opened up to her left and right, as she walked. She could disregard most of them – they were too small, too narrow, too low to allow a wolf to pass. A deep boom, like a roll of thunder, echoed around her – the first drumbeat. Eira quickened her pace.

She reached a fork in the path and stooped to examine the ground. There were paw prints leading left, and to her delight they seemed even, with no sign of dragging on the front paw. The wolf healers had clearly worked their magic.

The tunnel climbed and fell, and the drum beat once more. Two hours gone. Eira began to run. She splashed through puddles, and saw paw prints shining on the ground, still wet. It would not be long now. Another rumble scared her – but it was not a third drumbeat; this sound was incessant. She ran faster, her torch only showing her a few paces ahead, so she nearly didn't stop in time when a drop opened up before her.

Eira peered down. At the base of the rockfall was a cave full of the roaring of the sea. Pinpricks of daylight were streaming in from gaps in the roof, and Eira extinguished her torch. There was enough light to see a pool of seawater. Its surface bubbled and frothed, for in the pool, swimming joyfully, was the pale wolf.

CHAPTER TWELVE

Eira saw him sniff the air and lift his head in her direction, ears flicking. She ducked down. She would have to show herself eventually – you could not sneak up on a wolf – but she was not looking forward to this first encounter, before he realised she meant him no harm.

The wolf climbed from the pool and shook himself, water flying from his pale coat. With his fur slicked down, he was still enormous, but less threatening.

Eira took a deep breath, and stood up.

The wolf saw her immediately. He crouched, the cave filling with his growls, his hackles rising. Eira fixed her eyes on his, and began to approach. For him to trust her, he had to respect her. She had to show him she wasn't afraid.

But she was. Approaching an untamed wolf felt like the most unnatural thing in the world. The boulders rocked beneath her, but she slid down the drop, maintaining eye contact. He started forward, but he was feinting. It was a good sign. This meant he didn't see her as prey. He was curious.

Eira reached the bottom and came to a halt at the edge of the pool, so the water stretched between them. He stood across from her, growling energetically.

An image of her mother came to her then, playfighting her wolf Tej. When she wanted him to stop, her mother rolled on to her back, signalling she was no threat.

Eira crouched, her eyes fixed on the wolf, and knelt. He was still growling, but his ears were upright. He was interested in what she would do next. Eira lay down, still looking into his amber eyes.

The wolf cocked his head.

It was working. He stopped growling, and sank on to his belly.

Eira's heart leaped. She was doing it! She was taming a w—

Boom.

The drum sounded a third time, and the wolf reacted immediately. If Eira had blinked, she wouldn't have seen him coming. Luckily, she did, and had time to reach for a handful of sand. In two bounds, he was on her, pinning her with immense force, his jaws open above her throat. It was like being crushed by rocks, but Eira flung the sand into his face. He yelped, shifting just enough for Eira to roll away, gathering more sand, and leap to her feet.

She ran for the boulders, climbing on to one so she

stood higher than him, and spun around, sand in one hand, dagger in the other. As the wolf approached, slinking and growling, she remembered Ani's words. But she was not ready to give up.

'*Ruko!*' she shouted. *Stop.*

The wolf did not stop.

Eira bared her teeth, and growled.

The wolf hesitated.

Eira growled again, louder, waving the dagger like a claw.

The wolf stepped closer, and Eira threw more sand. He whined, and took a step back.

Eira jumped down from her boulder, and began to advance.

The wolf stepped back again.

Eira reached for a third handful of sand, and he retreated to the other side of the pool.

Eira stalked after it, spreading her arms to make herself bigger. They returned to their positions, staring at each other across the water. They stayed like this for a long, long time. Eira only knew how long when the *boom* of the drum came again. The wolf startled, but this time he paced a while, and then sat once more. Eira threw some meat across to him, and he sniffed then swallowed it gladly. She threw another piece, and another. He licked his lips. Another hour passed.

Seeing an opportunity, Eira threw back her own head and howled. The wolf copied her, and then whined, sinking to its haunches.

He was mirroring her. She lay down on her front and, questioning her life choices, put her face into the pool.

She braced herself for hot breath on her head, the awful press of paws on her back, tearing fangs at her neck – but when she looked up, the wolf had put his head in too, and was blowing bubbles through his nose. He was playing. He slid into the water, like a crocodile, and began to slowly paddle towards her, still blowing bubbles through his nose.

'What you're you doing, *budhoo*?'

He swam in slow circles, looking back at her, and Eira realised he was inviting her to play. She looked at the water, and squared her shoulders.

This is fine, she told herself. *Going for a dip with a sea wolf. Not a stupid idea at all.*

She left her dagger on the edge, and slid into the water. It was like tiny knives stabbing her skin, but this was why she had practised in her bath. She mastered her breath, and felt her body slowly burn as her nerves screamed, and then numbed. The wolf was watching, treading water. She searched it for signs of attack – lowered ears, bared fangs – but it was wide-eyed as if to say, *Who's the budhoo now?*

CHAPTER THIRTEEN

Eira stayed in the water as long as she could bear. The wolf, covered in its thick fur, was well suited to these freezing temperatures, but Eira began to shiver after ten minutes. She wished she could be in longer – the wolf was so relaxed and happy, and she had half a mind to try to approach him, to see if he would let her touch him. But she lost feeling in her feet and fingers, and was forced to clamber out, shivering so hard she almost fell, and crawling to her clothes.

She wiped as much water off her body as possible and dressed as quickly as she could. She huddled into a ball, clamping her hands under her armpits, and rocking back and forth, trying to heat herself up.

Her thoughts were slow and stupid. She'd stayed in too long. What a dumb way to die. She should stand up, run around, but that felt impossible. It would be much easier to lie down and go to sleep. At least the wolf wouldn't go hungry.

She lay down on the sand. It was hard and

uncomfortable, but she couldn't get up now. The sand was warmer. Soft, pillowy and thick. It was breathing.

No. That's not right. Eira heaved her eyelids open. It was the biggest effort in the world, but when she managed, she saw white, like snow. Could cold water make you blind? Feeling was returning to her fingers. She flexed them, and felt fur brush her palms.

The pale wolf was curled around her, warming her with his body heat. She could feel his breath lifting and lowering his ribcage, the slow and steady beat of his heart. She shifted so she could look at his head, laid on the ground to her right. His eyes were closed. He was asleep.

'Thank you,' she whispered, and his eyebrow twitched, an amber eye sliding open. She looked into his face and, slowly, carefully, lifted her hand so he could see it. His eyes latched on to it. She began to lower it towards his head. She felt the change in his breathing as fear set in, but for now, their bond held. She laid her hand gently between his ears, at the broad, soft point above his eyes. He let out a huge sigh, as though of relief, and unconsciously, Eira did the same.

Eira let him sleep until another drumbeat woke him. He whined and shifted, as though to go back to sleep, but she'd lost count now. Daylight was still streaming through the gaps above them, but she couldn't risk being late. She didn't know how willingly the wolf would follow her, and she was tired, hungry. It would be a slower return.

Carefully, she rolled away from him. The wolf sat up, watching her. She took out another piece of meat, and fed him. He ate from her hand. That was a good sign, but she didn't have enough to coax him all the way through the cave. She stood slowly, and walked towards the boulders. He stood up, his head tilted.

'Come on, *budhoo*. Time to go.'

She climbed the rockfall and groped for her torch, lighting it once more. The wolf was still in the cave, and Eira could hear him whining. She walked out of sight, and then went back to the edge. He'd come a little closer.

'Come on,' she repeated, holding out a piece of meat. She only had two left. He paced, wanting her to throw it. 'No,' she said. 'You have to come and get it.'

Slowly, haltingly, the wolf began to climb, checking for signs of a trap. He snarled at the torch when he reached the top, but Eira stood firm.

'I need this to see. You'll have to get used to it.'

He bent his head, and ate again from her palm, his sharp fangs whispering against her skin, his rough tongue rasping. Eira's own stomach growled. She'd not eaten since early that morning.

'Let's go,' she told him. She began to walk away. She could barely make him out. '*Jaldi*. We mustn't be late.'

Another drumbeat hit them as they reached the fork where Eira had turned left. How many hours was that? How long had she been asleep for? If only she had the energy to run. She stopped. Her body was still cold, her legs sore and heavy. The wolf trotted up to her, and sat down beside her, panting.

She looked at him, considering. 'What do you think, *budhoo*?'

He looked at her, tongue lolling, eyebrows twitching. Eira reached carefully out, and rubbed between his ears again. He closed his eyes, the purest sign of trust. Slowly, she slid her arm down, to his shoulders. He pressed into her, enjoying the scratches. She pushed her arm into his fur, and when he didn't react, she circled her other arm around his neck.

He stilled. His eyes were open, a growl at the base of his throat.

'It's all right,' she said, and pressed her forehead to his nose. It was cold, and wet. His breath was hot. He understood she was showing him respect, asking him a question. This time, when Eira encircled his neck with her arms, he didn't react. He let her push him down and swing her leg across his wide back.

'All right,' she said soothingly, to herself as much as him. She pulled herself upright, holding on to the thick ruff of his neck. He stood up so suddenly she cracked her head on the roof of the tunnel.

She muffled her cry of pain in her elbow, and pressed herself flat. '*Gods*. Let's see how this goes.'

She squeezed her heels into his sides, and to her amazement the wolf began to walk.

CHAPTER FOURTEEN

'I thought you weren't going to call attention to yourself!' said Kore, exasperated. 'I heard about the girl who rode the wolf out of the tunnel before you even got back here.'

Eira tried not to look smug. 'How was I to know I still had two hours left?'

'First person ever to ride their wolf out. First person back. Only five through to the final trial.' Kore shook her head. 'You're meant to be blending in.'

'No use,' said Eira, and told her about Ani.

Kore looked shocked. 'What if she's told your mother?'

'Nothing she can do from the Marbled Hills. Are they there yet?'

'I don't know,' snapped Kore. 'Haven't been able to use your blood bond, have I? Dev came again today. I think he's worried you're ill.'

'He won't come again before the trials are done now,' said Eira. 'Training starts tomorrow.'

Five days of training with their wolves, under the supervision of the judges. And then the final trial – to ride the sea wolf to the Sea Henge and back. It wasn't as simple as it sounded. The henge was five miles offshore, the currents were treacherous, and if your bond with your wolf wasn't strong enough, it might throw you off, ignore your instructions, or turn on you in the middle of the sea.

But Eira was already surer of her bond with the pale wolf than anything else in her life. When she'd ridden from the caves and up the sandstone staircase, the shock on Dev and the other judges' faces was a picture. Six Wolflings had had to be rescued, one was in a life-threatening condition, and over the remaining two hours only four others emerged.

Hajay was second after Eira, dragging his wolf by a rope. Ani had ordered him to release the wolf, as it had to follow willingly, and Eira had willed the animal to run away. But it had stayed, its eyes wide and fearful. Next were two boys, leading their wolves without ropes, and finally Meri, who walked beside the female wolf Eira had drugged. There was a claw mark on her cheek but she was alive.

The five successful Wolflings were asked to name their wolves, to help aid them in training. Hajay called his Ravi, Meri named hers Indra, and though she nearly said *budhoo,* Eira decided it was mean to label this beautiful creature a fool.

'Laddu,' she said.

'You're naming it after a type of sweet?' scoffed Hajay.

'Names are personal,' said Ani. 'You're free to use whichever you like, *Esta*.'

Eira took her point.

Kore made a harrumphing sound. 'Well, go on then, tell me the story.'

Eira yawned as she stood in the training pen, shoulder to shoulder with Meri and one of the other boys, whose name was Parth. Amma had insisted on waking her at the crack of dawn and fed her so much breakfast Eira was worried she'd fall asleep at training.

'Am I boring you, Esta?' snapped Dev.

'Sorry, Commander.'

'There will be no yawning. I need you alert, able, ready. We will be learning to groom our wolves today. This will build your bond, and get them used to human touch. Tomorrow, verbal commands. Stop, go, left, right and so on. Then we will work on wolf riding –' he glanced at Eira – 'and the *correct* way to sit.'

Hajay glowered. He had heard about Eira's success and was not happy about it.

'Then non-verbal commands, using posture and so on. On the fifth day, you will practise riding in the shallows. You will have one further day to use as you wish, and the final trial will take place on Samhain.'

'Commander.' Hajar had his hand up. 'When do we learn the other orders?'

'Such as?'

'Attack,' said Hajay, his eyes gleaming.

'That is reserved for your official Ryder training,' said Dev, looking disquieted. 'If there are no more questions, we will bring in your wolves.'

Eira's mood lightened at the sight of Laddu, and she was sure she didn't imagine him quickening his pace to reach her faster. Each of them stood beside their wolves. Ravi looked fearful beside Hajay, and Indra stared imperiously at Meri. Ani walked along the line, handing out brushes.

'Why do we have to do this?' said Hajay, wrinkling his nose.

Ani met his eyes coolly. Eira was glad to see she didn't hide her dislike. 'Because if you do not look after your wolf, how can you expect them to look after you?'

Eira loved brushing Laddu. His fur was revealed to be an even brighter shade, and his coat shone and crackled. Then they washed the wolves, and dried them with large mats made of woven rushes. Finally, they brushed them again, so that by the end of the first day the wolves looked worthy of the wolf queen's pack.

Dev nodded approvingly. 'Tomorrow the real work begins.'

CHAPTER FIFTEEN

Over the next four days, Eira learned not only commands and posture, but also how to read a wolf's body language, how to shift her weight when they were swimming (more central, to spread the weight) versus when they were running (further back, for balance). She and Laddu clearly had the strongest bond, though after the third day all the Wolflings had successfully mounted their wolves.

Meri was docile, almost subservient to Indra, Parth stayed calm no matter what, the other boy Cubi used a lot of encouragement, and Hajay used force. Eira wondered what they saw when they watched her and Laddu. She found it easy to read Laddu's moods, his needs, and in return he responded to the slightest touch, the quietest command. Eira loved it all.

It had rained much of the week, but the final day of training dawned bright and cold. They stood shivering on the beach. They gave their commands and the wolves crouched to allow them to climb on their backs.

'All right!' shouted Ani, over the wind. '*Ek, do, teen!*'

They urged their wolves forward and the five of them plunged into the waves, the cold lapping at their legs, the wolves swimming joyfully, in their natural habitat at last. Eira laughed happily.

When at last they climbed from the waves, drenched and exuberant, Dev had a twinkle in his eye.

'Now you see, don't you? A life on wolfback, at the service of the wolf queen . . . it's an honour so few can dream of, even fewer attain. One more trial, and you can start your life as a Ryder in earnest.'

The boys and Meri whooped, and Eira tried to hold on to the glee she'd felt. But whatever her future held, it was not training with the other Wolflings. Her mother would never let her become a Ryder.

I don't even want to be a Ryder. I only want to prove myself. And if my mother won't accept this means I deserve my freedom, I'll take it. And you, Laddu, you'll come with me.

'Tonight and tomorrow,' continued Dev, 'rest. Be with your loved ones. Come and see your wolves in the pens. And on Samhain, your final trial will begin.'

Ani drew Eira aside as the others left the beach, gesturing for one of the other judges to take Laddu. He whined, but Eira patted him and said, 'I'll come and see you tomorrow.'

Once they were alone, Ani moved closer to Eira. 'Don't react,' she said. 'The Forgiver is watching.'

Eira looked around, and spotted Kore at the mouth of her cave. 'Kore knows who I am. I made her help me.'

Ani looked surprised, but not angry. 'Maybe she knows more than me.'

'About what?'

But Ani was trudging away, towards Kore.

Kore walked out to meet them, her white hair whipping around her face.

'Forgiver,' said Ani deferentially, 'have you heard the news?'

'What news?' asked Kore warily.

'The wolf queen.' Ani looked between them. 'She's on her way back.'

'Has the trouble in the Marbled Hills already been dealt with?' asked Eira.

Ani shrugged. 'Must be. She's already in sight of the Isles.'

A chill ran through Eira. Her mother might be home before the final trial began. 'Why?'

'I was hoping you could tell me,' Ani said to Kore.

'I could read the blood bond,' Kore suggested.

'I hate being a pin cushion,' grumbled Eira, but she followed Kore into her cave, and presented her arm. Kore used her ceremonial dagger, and had Eira bleed on to the fishbones she kept for this purpose. Then she threw them on to her fire, waiting until they blackened and smoked, then snatched them out, dropping them to the ground.

'She is near,' said Kore. 'She will arrive the day after tomorrow.'

'What time?' asked Eira desperately.

'Does it look like a sundial to you?' snapped Kore, frowning down at the bones. 'She is worried, afraid. Something she has dreaded happening has happened, and she thought she had more time.' Kore looked up at Eira, her eyes fearful. 'Gods. Do you think she knows about you?'

'How could she?' said Eira. And anyway, surely her mother wouldn't turn around for her?

'I should go,' Ani said. 'I would think very carefully about continuing, Rajkumari. The most dangerous part is ahead.'

'Laddu will look after me.'

Ani sighed. 'If you want to prove yourself, there are other ways. I can vouch for your strengths.'

'I want to complete the trials,' said Eira.

'Then let's hope for your sake that your mother isn't too prompt,' said Ani, and left the cave.

Chapter Sixteen

The morning of Samhain arrived, and Seren did not. The castle of broken boats was empty behind them, everyone on the dunes to watch the final trial. Five Wolflings and their wolves stood on the beach, staring out at the sea.

It did not look good. All night a storm had raged, keeping everyone awake with rain so heavy it sounded like feet stamping on the hulls. In Kore's cave, the seawater pools swelled and sloshed. The thunder and lightning had passed but the sea was swollen and angry-looking. On a calm, clear day, you could see the henge from shore. Now it was impossible to see further than the waves cresting right in front of them.

Ravi whined, and Hajay slapped him on the muzzle. Laddu put his nose in Eira's headscarf, and she rubbed his ruff. In some ways, she was grateful for the weather. It meant hiding her face was not so strange; Amma would be in the crowd this time.

'Wolflings,' said Dev, his voice carried away by the

wind, 'you have tracked your wolf, tamed your wolf – now we must see if you have trained them. A ten-mile journey on wolfback, to the fabled Sea Henge. You must place your mark upon one of the stones, as generations of Ryders have before you.

'You are alone out there but for your wolf. You must be as brave as your wolves, and they can only be as brave as you.'

Meri's teeth were chattering. Hajay's eyes were fixed on the horizon.

Eira spoke into Laddu's ear. 'We got this, boy. You've got me, and I've got you.'

Laddu nuzzled into her shoulder.

'*Ek . . .*' began Dev, and the Wolflings swung themselves up on to their wolves. The crowd began to cheer. '*Do . . . teen!*'

Hajay shouted as he hit Ravi's haunch, and Meri urged Indra on. Eira leaned forward and Laddu began to run, and plunged into the waves.

The current hit them instantly, pulling them violently out to sea. As they surfaced, Eira felt Laddu's panic and suppressed her own. 'Gently, boy. We need to get clear of the break. Swim with the current.'

She pulled on his ruff to guide him, and he began to swim. Another wave hit them but he carried on, paddling faster, until the steeply sloping ground dropped off and the waves lessened. Ahead of them, Meri and Indra were making good progress. Eira looked back. She could see someone alone in the water, someone without their wolf. It was Cubi. But then she saw Ani on wolfback, swimming towards him, her scarlet cloak billowing behind her.

Hajay and Ravi broke through a wave, Parth and his wolf close behind. Four left.

It was like being on a very fast, very splashy boat – or at least Eira imagined so. She'd never been on a boat before, apart from being birthed on one. The current swept them out at a terrifying rate, the waves no longer jagged but rolling. Eira saw Meri bend over Indra's side a couple of times to throw up, and thought that a seasick Ryder would not be much use at all.

Hajay stayed behind her, but Parth was dropping back. Eira realised that Hajay was following her route, Ravi swimming in their slipstream, making it easy for him to avoid the riptides and small whirlpools that dotted this treacherous stretch.

After a couple of hours, the Sea Henge came into view. The sight filled Eira's chest with pride. Henges were an essential part of Isles lore, placed there by druids of old for ceremonies and ancient rites. Her mother was obsessed by henges and had built her castle to be close to this one.

A shout pulled her from her thoughts. She hadn't noticed the splashing forms ahead. But now she saw Meri and Indra were in trouble.

They'd been pulled north of the henge, but, worse still, they were spinning in a jerky, unnatural fashion.

They'd been caught by a whirlpool.

'Go, Laddu!' shouted Eira, and the wolf obeyed, making for Meri and Indra. By the time they reached them, Indra had thrown Meri off, and was swimming clear of the current, but Meri was still spinning, approaching the dead zone of the centre, where a rip would carry her straight down and pin her in place.

'*Jaldi!*' Eira urged, and fearlessly, trustingly, Laddu threw himself into the swirling pool. Eira held on tight as it took them at nauseating speed. Laddu did not falter as he forced his way to Meri, whose hands were just visible as she kicked with all her might against the sucking current.

As Eira spluttered, spitting out seawater, she saw Meri's head emerge, her eyes wide and terrified, choking. And then she slipped beneath the surface, and did not come up.

CHAPTER SEVENTEEN

'No!' shouted Eira, but Laddu had seen Meri vanish too. He dived, and Eira held on tighter as she was plunged into a whirling world of bubbles and sickening pressure. She tried to open her eyes but they felt like they might pop. Her ears ached, her lungs burned, and then—

Then they were rising, Laddu swimming free of the tug of the whirlpool, and as they surfaced Eira saw he had Meri's arm clasped gently in his jaws. The girl was vomiting seawater, her eyes rolling. But she was alive.

'You did it, Laddu!' cried Eira, and reached for Meri. She dragged her up on to Laddu's back in front of her, and Meri collapsed over the wolf's neck, taking deep, dragging breaths. Her first gasping word was 'Indra?'

'Safe,' said Eira, patting her back. She checked behind her. 'Swimming to shore.'

With a heavy heart, Eira began to turn Laddu to follow.

'No!' spluttered Meri. 'Keep going. You can complete the trial.'

Eira looked doubtfully at her. 'I think you should see a healer.'

'It can wait,' said Meri feebly. 'Please, I'll feel terrible otherwise. I already stole your wolf.'

It took Eira a moment to process what she'd said. 'You knew?'

'I followed you,' she said. 'Well, I followed Ish. He was easy to track. I saw your trick with the valerian, and was going to copy you, but then I saw you didn't go after Indra. So I did. I feel really bad,' said Meri, plaintively. 'So please, keep going.'

'It might be too much for Laddu,' said Eira. Fully grown and trained wolves could carry two adults, but cubs were only meant to carry one child.

'I would offer to swim,' said Meri. 'But . . .'

Eira groaned. 'Why did you try to become a Ryder if you can't swim?'

'My father—'

'You know, I think the world would be a better place if more children disobeyed their parents.'

But Laddu was treading water, panting happily, seeing it all as a great adventure. Eira felt a surge of love for the wolf. 'You want to try, boy?' she murmured, and Laddu whined excitedly.

She turned them once more for the henge. Hajay had not stopped to help them, though he must have seen what was happening; he was far ahead.

'*Jaldi*,' she said, and Laddu ploughed after him.

'He's fast!' shouted Meri. She was shaking, but then she began to laugh, and Eira, on the edge of terror, joined in. They stopped abruptly when they reached the stones.

The sea seemed to settle around them, though surely it should be choppy. The water was glassy, pond-still, the whittled tree trunks and the pointed shards of granite reflected so the sea and sky were infinite mirrors of each other.

Hajay had marked a stone – the biggest, of course – drawing his snake over older marks. He was crossing the centre of the henge, and Eira watched as he took both hands off Ravi's ruff, and pressed his palms hard into his ears. Ravi's eyes shot wide, his ears flattening. Both wolf and boy were staring into the middle distance.

'Hajay! What're you doing?'

But the boy didn't answer, and as they broke the ring of the henge, Laddu halted, as though swimming into an invisible net. He whined, and backed away. 'What is it, Laddu?' asked Eira.

'Esta, look!' Meri was pointing, her voice full of horror.

Eira looked back at Hajay and Ravi, and gasped.

Blood was streaming from Hajay's nose, red spreading in a cloud through the water.

'Hajay!' Eira shouted. 'What's happening? Ravi! Move!'

But neither of them did, and when Eira tried to manoeuvre Laddu back towards them, he again halted outside the henge. Eira felt she had no choice. She slid off Laddu's back, and into the calm water.

The moment she broke the boundary, she felt she'd slipped through to the other side of a mirror. The space beyond the henge felt indistinct, unimportant. There was silence around her, not even her strokes through the water making sound, and then, as she entered the bloodied water, there came a high, awful, mesmerising sound. Music. She felt it rather than heard it in the marrow of her bones, in the chambers of her heart, the nerves beneath her skin.

'Hajay,' she called weakly, holding on to the boy's leg. 'Hajay, move.'

It would be so easy to let herself sink. But she remembered the cold sickness after swimming in the cave pool, and Laddu's warmth calling her back. *No*, she thought to herself. *Stay*.

She hit Hajay's leg, hard. She pinched him, harder. He didn't respond, too lost in the sound. Eira kept herself tethered above it by thinking of Laddu, of Amma, of Kore, but it was overwhelming, filling her soul with a sort of dread. She had to act fast.

She swam around to Ravi's haunches, and kicked him. Nothing. Not knowing what else to do, she placed her feet on his haunches, took hold of his tail, and yanked with all her might.

Ravi howled in pain, and started forward. He

swam straight for Laddu, breaking the henge. But Hajay hadn't held on. Eira turned him on his back, gripped him under the chin, and swam desperately for the boundary. Meri helped her haul him on to Laddu's back. He was large and heavy, and Laddu whined.

'I know, boy,' said Eira, still treading water. 'But we can't leave him.'

She stared helplessly after Ravi, who was swimming towards shore. She couldn't blame the wolf for abandoning Hajay, but now she was stuck. Laddu couldn't carry them all, and Eira's arms already ached. The dread from the music still sat in her bones. Hajay was a dead weight, and she and Meri tied him on to Laddu's back with their ropes.

'What happened?' asked Meri fearfully, and Eira shook her head. She didn't have the breath to explain. If they were going to have a chance, they had to leave now.

'Come on, Laddu,' she said to her wolf. 'Let's swim together.'

'Your mark,' said Meri, and Eira remembered her belt, the dye in the pouch. But she didn't have time. Every moment Laddu's and her own strength would wane. Eira undid her belt and let it sink, dagger and all, to the sea bed. An offering. A sacrifice. A chance at survival.

They turned for the shore, the castle out of sight behind the waves, an impossible distance. But what else could they do?

'Ready, Laddu?'

His white muzzle touched her cheek. Eira took a deep breath, and began to swim.

CHAPTER EIGHTEEN

Eira thought they would make it. They were maybe halfway back to shore, and Eira could make out the indistinct shape of the castle on the horizon when waves lifted them up. But then a cramp gripped her right leg. She screamed in pain, and Laddu whined and swam closer. Meri bent to pull her up, but Eira shook her head.

'Laddu can't carry us all,' she said through gritted teeth. 'You go.'

'We can't leave you,' said Meri fearfully.

'Tell them I need help.'

'It'll be hours,' said Meri. 'I can try to swim—'

'No,' snapped Eira. 'You can't.'

Eira was using Laddu's ruff to support herself, and could feel him fighting to keep them afloat. Gods, she hated Hajay. She hated the trials, and the Ryders, and Meri. Most of all, she hated her mother. Did she know about the deadly music at the henge?

The cramp released its grip, but Eira's leg still

throbbed. There was no way she could swim so far. Her best chance was to float, and hope they would come soon.

'Meri, go. Ani will come and get me. Tell her Eira needs her to come.'

Meri frowned. 'Eira?'

'Go,' said Eira, swimming up to Laddu's muzzle. He was panting, his head hot as she rested her own briefly against it. 'You have to go, boy, all right?' He whined. 'I know. But I'll see you onshore. Please. This is the only way.'

She gave him the command, and though unwilling, he went.

Watching him go was the loneliest moment of Eira's life. She felt cracked open, alive to how alone she had been for so long. And she didn't want to go back to being stone again. Whatever punishment her mother chose, Eira would insist on having Laddu with her. He was her wolf, and she was his. Surely her mother would understand that.

She lay on her back and let herself float, kicking every so often to stay in the same place, checking her location by the distance to shore, the position of the castle. So many thoughts tumbled through her head. She had failed the final trial. She had told Meri her real name. Her mother was on her way home. But, above all, she thought about the terrible music. What had caused it? The way it had affected Hajay, Ravi and Laddu, the way it had gnawed into Eira, felt unearthly.

But that wasn't quite right. It felt entirely of the earth, so that they became the unnatural ones. Trespassers.

Eira was used to being left with her thoughts. She recited her Hellenic alphabet, her Mother Realm chants. She hummed aloud the songs of the Ural Mountains, and then, over her own voice and the sloshing of the sea, she heard the steady parting of the water around a wolf. Eira smiled in relief – but the smile slid off her face.

It was not Ani coming to get her. It was not even Dev.

It was her mother.

Seren was scary enough in person – but on wolfback, she was otherworldly. Her face was set with a scowl so deep it looked engraved, and Tej, her wolf, matched her expression, glaring at her. They swam closer, closer, until Tej drew up alongside her and her mother stared down at her, her long black hair flying. She was still in her war sari – she must have come straight to the sea upon her return.

Eira wondered who had betrayed her, Ani or Kore? Or perhaps Seren had heard Meri say her real name. It didn't really matter. Eira knew she was in the most trouble she'd ever been in in her life.

Her mother held out a hand, and hauled Eira roughly up behind her.

'Hi, Mother,' said Eira into her back.

'It is better,' she said in their mother tongue, so she knew she was really in trouble, 'if you do not speak.'

*

They reached the shore within an hour. The current and tide must have carried Eira closer. The beach was thronged with people, their shouts as they saw them carried out to them by the wind. Eira peered around her mother, hoping to catch sight of Laddu. But he was not there, and nor were the other wolves and Wolflings. They must have been taken to the healers. She saw Kore at her cave mouth, Amma at the front of the crowd, kneeling and tearing at her hair, wailing. As soon as they dismounted, Amma splashed into the shallows and hugged Eira tight.

'Rajkumari, *meri jaan*, my child!'

'Away, Roopa,' snapped Seren, taking Eira's wrist in a vice-like grip, and pulling her away from the crowd. She was dragged past Ani, who spread her hands as if to say, *I did warn you*. People were calling out terms of respect to her mother, but she pulled Eira all the way to the concealed mouth of a tunnel, where Ryders stood aside to let them past. They walked directly to her throne room, where her mother threw Eira's wrist away from her as though she were something rotting.

They faced each other, the wolf queen and her daughter, and Eira could see why the myths about her mother claimed she was half woman, half wolf. She looked utterly wild with anger, but there was a containment to her. She would pounce only when it most suited her.

'I suppose I should thank you for coming to get me,' said Eira, deciding she had to puncture the tension, but her mother's nostrils flared. 'Did Laddu get back all right? He's the pale wolf, the one I tamed.'

She hoped the mention of the wolf would soften her mother, but it seemed to do the opposite. Her mouth formed a thin tight line, and then she said, voice shaking, 'It is not all right. He is dead.'

CHAPTER NINETEEN

A ringing started in Eira's ears. 'What?'

'His heart gave out in the shallows. He reached the shore, and the Ryders were able to rescue the children. But the wolf was beyond saving. He will be given full ceremonial rites, as is his due.'

'No,' said Eira. Her legs gave way at last, and she fell to her knees. 'You're lying.'

She longed for this to be a lie, a punishment. But she knew not even Seren was capable of such malice.

'I wish I were.' Did her mother's voice crack? She loved the wolves, and felt their losses as keenly as the death of any person. Perhaps more. 'He was not strong enough.'

Eira broke down. She pressed her face into her hands, and wailed. Laddu was dead, and it was all her fault. She had made him carry Meri and Hajay, had left him to battle the fierce currents alone. Her heart felt like it was literally breaking into pieces, shattering like a pane of glass.

She felt a hand, warm and strong, on her shoulder. She began to shake uncontrollably, and a blanket was wrapped around her. She struggled to push it off. She didn't want to be warm when Laddu was cold. But her mother wrapped her arms around her and the blanket, and held on tight.

Eira could not remember the last time her mother had held her. She hated her, but she needed her, and she clung on, weeping until she had no tears left. Eventually, Eira pushed away from her mother, and leaned heavily against the wall, her eyes sore and blurry.

Her mother stayed crouched before her, and on her face was an expression she'd never worn while looking at her daughter. Pity. Understanding.

Eira didn't want it, any of it. She wanted Laddu back.

'Do you have any idea what you've done?'

Eira's anger reared as suddenly as a snake. 'I've taken what is rightfully mine. What is rightfully anyone's. My freedom. Or maybe you've forgotten that, collecting countries like trophies.'

'How dare you—'

'No!' shouted Eira, wild with grief. 'How dare you!' Her voice echoed off the walls. 'How dare you treat me like a secret, a prisoner—'

'It was for your own safety—'

'No! It was for yours, so it would seem like you had no weakness. Well, you failed, because I know

77

you don't love me. You only love your wolves, and your Ryders, and your realms. You can let me go!' But even as she said it, Eira felt all her strength leave her. Where was there to go, without her wolf? 'I loved him,' she sobbed. 'And it's my fault he's dead.'

'You know I understand how that feels. My first wolf died—'

'I'm nothing like you! You don't understand me!'

'Unfortunately for both of us, I do,' said her mother firmly. 'I see so much of myself in you, Eira—'

'I don't want to hear it!'

Her mother's beautiful face closed over. She rose to her feet.

'That's right,' sneered Eira, wanting to hurt her. 'Lock me up again. Put me out of the way. You never even wanted me.'

'No!' shouted her mother, making Eira flinch. 'I walked through fire to have you. I wanted you more than anything in this world. All I have built, I have built so that you can inherit it.'

'You build for your own glory.'

'I build so my power is absolute, and nothing can harm you.' Her face crumpled. 'Why did you do something so stupid, so dangerous? Freedom is not everything.'

Eira saw in her mother's face that she didn't really believe that.

'You're tired,' she said. 'And Amma is frantic. But what happened at the henge? The boy said he heard music. Dev assumed he was hallucinating.'

'No,' said Eira stonily. 'I heard it too.'

Her mother hadn't expected this. 'What did it sound like?'

'Let me have a question. Why did you come back?'

'Thane Boreal is on the move,' said her mother, so quickly Eira knew she was lying, or telling a half-truth. Eira waited, and her mother sighed. 'There was a quake, in the Suthridge. A small one. But it uncovered a henge. It threw out the alignment. I must recalculate.'

'Recalculate what?'

'What did the music sound like?' her mother said, ignoring her question.

Eira described it. Even talking about it made her feel sick.

Her mother nodded. 'It's awake,' she said.

'What is?'

She looked into Eira's face. 'The earth music. We're running out of time.' She crossed to the tunnel door, and knocked twice. Ani opened it and entered, cautiously.

'Take my daughter back to her chamber. Don't let her out of your sight. And send the scholars. Immediately.'

'I want to stay—'

'You do not give the orders here,' said her mother, implacable. 'This cannot wait.'

And Ani led Eira from the room.

CHAPTER TWENTY

Dazed, Eira walked through the tunnels. When they were halfway to her chamber Ani stopped and turned.

'I'm so sorry about Laddu,' she said, and her eyes were full of tears. 'He was not in pain at the end. He was not afraid.'

'But I wasn't there,' said Eira, her voice breaking.

'I was.' Ani rested a hand on her shoulder, but Eira pulled away.

'Did Ravi survive? Parth, and Cubi?'

'Yes.'

'Hajay will be a Ryder,' said Eira dejectedly.

Ani shook her head fiercely. 'He wouldn't have been allowed to train, even if he'd reached us on his own wolf. It is at our discretion who joins.'

'I don't suppose a princess can.'

'No,' said Ani sadly. 'I don't think that would be allowed.'

'I only wanted to be free.'

'Give it time,' said Ani. 'Your mother will hear

of your courage, your strength. Perhaps things will change.'

Eira was not convinced. Ani began to walk again, but Eira pulled on her elbow. 'What's earth music?'

Ani flinched. 'It's worth more than my life to tell you,' she said. Eira glared, and she relented. 'Listen, there's a power greater than any living thing has ever possessed. Thane Boreal is searching for it, and so is your mother. That's all I know.'

'But that's only half a story,' said Eira frustratedly.

'Only your mother knows the full one.'

Eira made a promise to herself, then. She would stay until she knew the whole story. And then she would leave this place, and take this power her mother so desired. Then maybe her mother would take her seriously. Then, maybe, Laddu wouldn't have died in vain.

Her guts twisted as she thought of her wolf. In many ways, it was the closest bond she'd ever had, with anyone or anything.

Waiting in her chamber was Amma. She'd been crying, and she clutched Eira tightly as Ani backed out of the room.

'*Meri jaan*, why? Why did you do such a dangerous thing? Why did you lie to me?'

Eira wriggled free. 'Would you have let me compete?'

'Of course not.'

She stared at Amma coolly. 'Then there is your answer.'

'I am here to protect you.' Amma stroked her cheek, as she had so many times before.

'No, you are my keeper.'

Amma flinched. Her gentle eyes filled with tears again. 'You're tired. I'll let you sleep. Do you want some warm milk and turmeric?'

Eira turned away. 'No.'

She heard Amma leave, locking the door behind her. Eira went straight to the grate, and hurried to Kore.

The Forgiver was expecting her. 'Gods,' she said as Eira tumbled from the tunnel. 'I thought your mother might have killed you.'

'Did she punish you?'

Kore shook her head. 'A telling off is all. She knew it was your idea. What did she say to you?'

But Eira was not there to gossip. She strode past Kore, and out into the darkness. Night had fallen heavy and star-filled, the moon pressing close to the ground.

She could hear Kore coming after her, rushing to keep up. 'Where are you going? If you get caught again . . .'

But the beach was empty. Eira walked north, to the burial grounds. There she saw Laddu's pelt shining in the darkness, like a fallen moon. A lump filled her throat. So it was true. She placed her hand on his soft fur. She imagined him as a cub, a small slice of starlight. She hoped there was an afterworld, and he would be happy there.

After a long time, Kore's thin arm slid around her. 'Oh, Eira, I'm so sorry.'

Eira let her friend hold her, clinging as tightly as she had to Laddu. But Kore was still here. And that would have to be enough.

Eira stood and pressed a final kiss to Laddu's cold muzzle. 'Goodbye, Laddu. In the next life, the next world, I will not fail you.'

'Eira, you didn't fail.' Kore's voice was tight, but she didn't cry. She never cried.

'I did,' said Eira, looking up at the moon. 'But I promise you, I promise him, I promise the sun and the stars, I will take my freedom. One way or another, I will leave this place, and not come back.'

Kore slid her hand into Eira's. 'I'll come with you,' she whispered. 'When you're ready, I'll come too.'

The girls stood beneath the infinite sky, before the vast sea, where out of sight, unnoticed by their ears, the earth music went on, writing their future, and the futures of every living thing, waiting for its moment to be heard.

THE GEOMANCER TRILOGY

BOOK 1

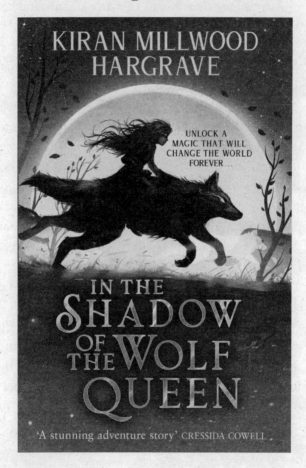

KIRAN MILLWOOD
HARGRAVE

UNLOCK A
MAGIC THAT WILL
CHANGE THE WORLD
FOREVER...

IN THE
SHADOW
OF THE WOLF
QUEEN

'A stunning adventure story' CRESSIDA COWELL

KIRAN MILLWOOD HARGRAVE

THE STORM AND THE SEA HAWK

'A stunning adventure story' CRESSIDA COWELL

BOOK 3, THE SHIP OF STRAYS,
COMING AUGUST 2025

Also by Kiran Millwood Hargrave

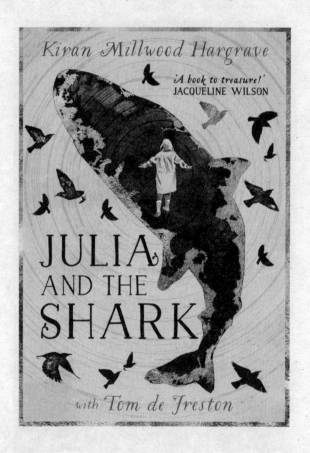

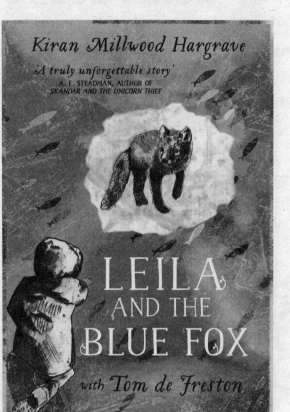

Kiran Millwood Hargrave

'A truly unforgettable story'
A. F. STEADMAN, AUTHOR OF
SKANDAR AND THE UNICORN THIEF

LEILA
AND THE
BLUE FOX

with *Tom de Freston*

HAPPY WORLD BOOK DAY

Choosing to read in your free time can help make you:

Feel happier

Better at reading

More successful

Whether it's **comics**, **audiobooks**, **recipe books** or **non-fiction** you can visit your school, local library or nearest bookshop for your next read.

Keep the reading fun going by **swapping** this book, **talking** about it, or **reading it again!**

Discover more at worldbookday.com

World Book Day® is a charity sponsored by National Book Tokens.

KIRAN MILWOOD HARGRAVE is an award-winning, bestselling novelist. Her debut story for children, *The Girl of Ink & Stars*, won the Waterstones Children's Book Prize, and the British Book Awards Children's Book of the Year. Her work has been short- and long-listed for numerous major prizes including the Costa Award and the Carnegie Award, and her novel *Julia and the Shark*, illustrated by Tom de Freston, was shortlisted for the Wainwright Prize and named Waterstones Children's Gift of the Year. *Leila and the Blue Fox*, also with Tom, won the Wainwright Prize. She's a graduate of both Oxford and Cambridge Universities, and lives in Oxford with her husband, daughter and cats, in a house between a river and a forest.